Curious George

Builds an Igloo

Adaptation by Erica Zappy
Based on the TV series teleplay
written by Kathy Waugh

SCHOLASTIC INC.

ISBN 978-0-545-67629-8

Curious George® television series merchandise © 2013 Universal Studios. Curious George® and related characters, created by Margret and H. A. Rey, are copyrighted and registered by Houghton Mifflin Harcourt Publishing Company and used under license. Licensed by Universal Studios Licensing LLC. All rights reserved. Published by Scholastic Inc., 557 Broadway, New York, NY 10012, by arrangement with Houghton Mifflin Harcourt Publishing Company. The PBS® Kids logo is a registered trademark of PBS® and is used with permission. SCHOLASTIC and associated logos are trademarks and/or registered trademarks of Scholastic Inc.

12 11 10 9 8   16 17 18/0

Printed in the U.S.A.   40

First Scholastic printing, December 2013

Design by Afsoon Razavi

It was a beautiful winter morning.
George was up early.

Next door, his friend Bill was up too!
Bill was building a house out of snow.
"It's called an igloo," Bill said. "I'm
going to sleep in it tonight."

George wanted to help.
He also wanted to sleep in the igloo!
It would be a lot of fun.

George tried stacking some blocks
of snow.
It was not easy.
They kept slipping and sliding.

"First, you make a circle in the snow," said Bill. "The snow blocks go around the circle. This makes a sturdy base for more snow blocks to go on top."

Bill showed George how to stack
snow blocks on top of the base.
Around and around they went until
there was only a hole left at the top.

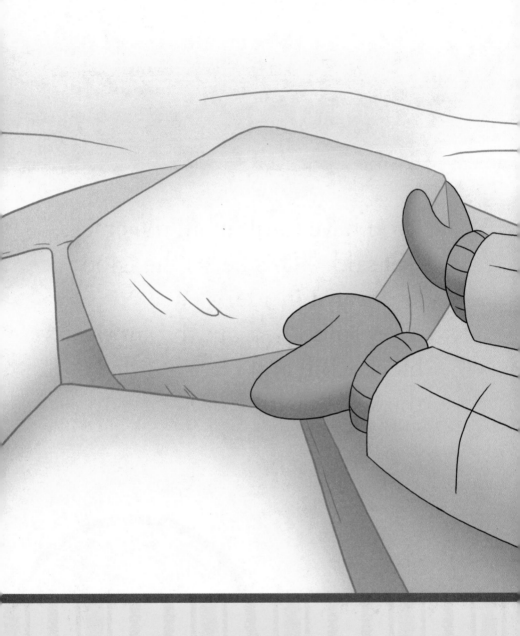

"The last piece is called the keystone," Bill said. "It keeps all the other snow blocks in place."

"You have to fill in all the cracks," Bill said. "This keeps the igloo nice and warm inside."
They smoothed out the snow blocks. Bill and George filled all the spaces with snow.

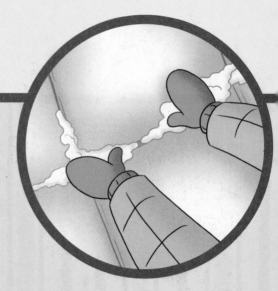

George was impressed.
But Bill's igloo was a little small.

George wanted to build his own igloo! A big igloo that could fit his bed and some friends and maybe a party with music . . .

George got to work.
This time he made the circle bigger!
He stacked the snow blocks around and
around, just as Bill had taught him.

George worked on his igloo until
the sun went down. It was a big
igloo. It even had a window!
But George was a tired monkey.
He did not have time to fill all
the cracks with snow.

The man with the yellow hat helped
move George's warm bed into the igloo.
George bundled up and went to sleep.

Soon George woke up.
He was very cold.
The window was drafty.
The cracks were letting the cold air in.

George really wanted to spend the
night in an igloo.
What could he do?
Then George had an idea!

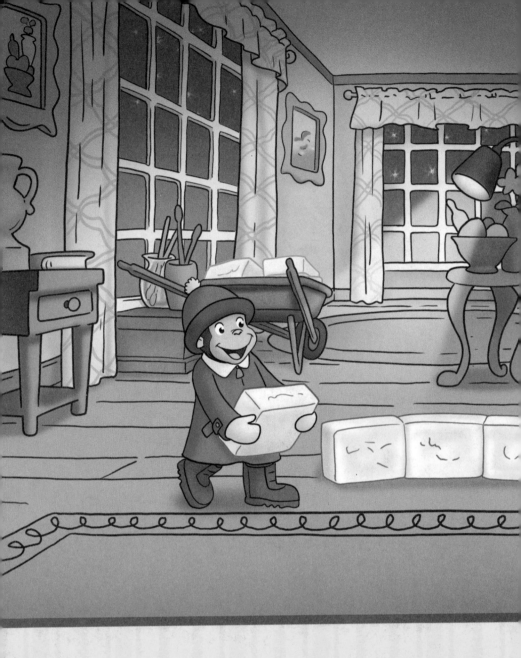

The man had told George to come inside
if he got cold. So George worked quickly
and built a new igloo in his living room!
It was nice and warm inside the house.

He crawled into his new
igloo and went to sleep . . . again.
The living room was the perfect
temperature for sleeping.
But it was too warm for a house made
of snow.
George's indoor igloo began to melt.

When George woke up the next
morning, his igloo had melted!
It had turned into a big puddle —
and a big mess to clean up.

Lucky for George, his outdoor igloo
was still standing.
The big igloo was too cold for sleeping,
but it was just right for a party.

George and his friends spent
the whole winter playing in his
big igloo, until it melted away
in the spring.

Build Your Own Igloo

Did you know that the word *igloo* means "snow house"? Eskimos have been building igloos for centuries, and now you can build your own mini igloo right in your kitchen! Ask a parent or another grownup for help.

You'll need mini marshmallows, one big marshmallow, pretzel sticks, and a piece of paper or paper plate. Draw a circle on your piece of paper to make the base for your igloo, just like George did.

Put the first layer of mini marshmallows around the circle. Then, use pretzel sticks to attach a second row of marshmallows on top: break the pretzel stick in half and push it into the bottom marshmallow. Push the next marshmallow onto the other side of the pretzel stick and  continue to build around this way. Stagger the marshmallows as you build upwards, moving each row in toward the center of the igloo as you go. Then start filling in the top of your igloo. Attach the big marshmallow to the front at the bottom of your igloo—this will be the entrance. If you want, you can decorate your igloo by adding a flag to the top!

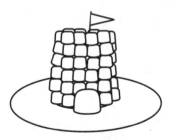

There are even great videos online to teach you how to build marshmallow igloos—ask a grownup to find one and see what other fun houses you can build!

*You could also use vanilla frosting as a type of glue in place of the pretzel sticks.

Melt Away

Some things melt when they get warm, just like George's indoor igloo. When something melts it changes into a liquid. Did you know ice melts into water at 32 degrees Fahrenheit?

Can you pick out which of the things below will melt if they get too warm?

Answers: The things that melt are an ice cube, ice cream, a snowman, candles, chocolate, and butter.